48 Grasshopper Estates

written by
Sara de Waal

illustrated by
Erika Medina

annick press
toronto • berkeley

Sicily Bridges lived at 48 Grasshopper Estates.

In all her years there, she had never seen one grasshopper, or, come to think of it, any grass.

That was alright with Sicily. She could make them herself.

Sicily Bridges could make almost anything.

When she needed a snack, she made chocolate chunk cookies with mint swirls.

When it was too quiet, she invented a trumpinette.

When she was scared, she created a dragon with seven tails that could terrify even the most fearsome closet monster.

And just in case that didn't work, she knew how to make a getaway boat that could sail right across the ocean.

Well, sort of.

On Thursday morning, Sicily's mum tiptoed to the side of her bed. Skirt swish, forehead kiss, and off to work she went.

Soon, the smell of Mrs. Rubenstein's oatmeal came wafting in, and with it came ideas:

a lake submarine, a unicorn castle painted aqua and pink,

and best of all,
a spaceship that
could take her to
Mars, with a
built-in supersonic
sandwich maker,
of course.

They were splendid ideas,
and as the sun rose, Sicily jotted
each one down in her notebook.

At seven o'clock came a knock at the door.

Ratta-tatta-tat. Tatta-ratta-ratta-tat.

"What will you make today?" asked Mrs. Rubenstein.

Sicily scanned her list.

Lake submarines were on the small side, but
they still needed at least two crew members.

A unicorn castle would be spectacular,
but how would she defend it all by herself?

And a supersonic sandwich maker would be perfect for her trip to Mars, but even she might need help eating all those sandwiches.

Sicily added one more thing to the list.

"An excellent choice," said Mrs. Rubenstein, and she left Sicily Bridges to her work.

Sicily made a fuzzy friend, a freckle-speckled friend, and a friend with four very fine toes.

She gave one friend suspenders for his too-big pants, and for another, she made glasses that were as red and round as Mars itself.

Sicily made a friend with ears so big he could hear snails talking at the bottom of the ocean.

Well, sort of.

At half past twelve came a knock at the door.

Ratta-tatta-tat. Tatta-ratta-ratta-tat.

"Have you made a friend?" asked Mrs. Rubenstein.

"Several," said Sicily.

"Would they like some sandwiches?" asked Mrs. Rubenstein.

"You know, it's the strangest thing," said Sicily. "These friends all prefer soup. But I'll take a peanut butter and cheese if you don't mind."

"An excellent choice," said Mrs. Rubenstein, and she left Sicily Bridges to her work.

Sicily gathered and sorted and painted and glued.

She made a checkered friend and a polka-dotted friend, and a friend with three perfectly placed ponytails.

For one friend she made a ruby-rimmed crown, and for another she made a hat as yellow as a field of sunflowers.

Sicily made a friend with arms so long
he could water flowers on the moon.

Well, sort of.

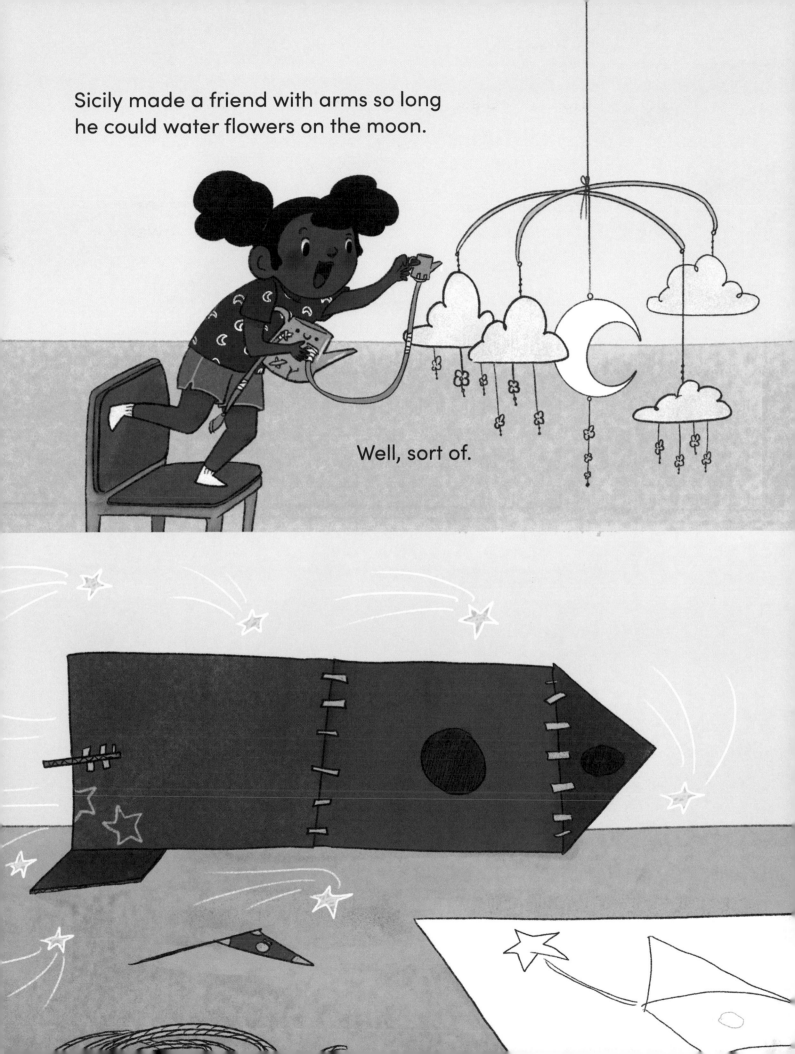

At two o'clock came a knock at the door.

Ratta-tatta-tat. Tatta-ratta-ratta-tat.

"What wonderful friends you have made," said Mrs. Rubenstein.

But Sicily only sighed. "They'll never make it to Mars," she said. "They are all afraid of heights."

"Oh dear," said Mrs. Rubenstein. "Do you think we ought to bring them down to the first floor?"

"It's no use," said Sicily. "Maybe none of these friends are good friends for me."

She joined Mrs. Rubenstein
at the window and peered down.

There, on his balcony, was Mr. Clipper
of apartment 8, wearing his pajamas
and eating a bowl of—

"Soup," said Sicily.

Suddenly, she knew just what to do.

Ratta-tatta-tat. Tatta-ratta-ratta-tat.

The door creaked open. "What do you want?" growled Mr. Clipper.

"Would you like a friend?" asked Sicily.

"A what?" asked Mr. Clipper.

Sicily picked up the friend with glasses. "A friend," she repeated.

Mr. Clipper frowned. "Does he like tomato soup?"

"I'm afraid that's all he eats," said Sicily.

"Well then," said Mr. Clipper. He tucked the friend with glasses under one arm and firmly closed the door.

"A perfect fit," said Mrs. Rubenstein.

For the rest of the afternoon, Sicily Bridges delivered friends to the residents of Grasshopper Estates, and Mrs. Rubenstein helped.

It turned out Mr. Corban knew a thing or two about suspenders.

And Mr. Drissell had need of a friend with big ears.

To Mrs. Stelpstra they gave the freckle-speckled friend, and when Miss Stavropoulos caught sight of a certain yellow hat, she was reminded of a field of sunflowers.

Mr. Boxum's window box was not as far away as the moon, but the long-armed friend was a first-rate flower waterer all the same.

Well, sort of.

In no time at all,
the cart was empty, and
Sicily felt a bit empty, too.

Ratta-tatta-tat. Tatta-ratta-ratta-tat.

There on the other side of the door stood a boy with very striped socks.

"Pardon me," said Sicily, "but are you going to space?"

"I was planning to," said the boy, "but I'm afraid my blaster-offer is broken."

"I just might have an extra one of those," said Sicily.

"Where exactly are you going?"

"Mars," said the boy.

"An excellent choice," said Mrs. Rubenstein.
"Do you have room for one more?"

It was the perfect fit.

Well, sort of.

For all my students, who often hear my stories first.
—S.D.

To Lalo and my dad.
—E.M.

Cover art by Erika Medina, designed by Paul Covello
Interior design by Paul Covello
Edited by Claire Caldwell

Annick Press Ltd.

We acknowledge the support of the Canada Council for the Arts and the Ontario Arts Council, and the participation of the Government of Canada/la participation du gouvernement du Canada for our publishing activities.

Library and Archives Canada Cataloguing in Publication

Title: 48 Grasshopper Estates / written by Sara de Waal ; illustrated by Erika Medina.
Other titles: Forty-eight Grasshopper Estates
Names: De Waal, Sara, 1990- author. | Medina, Erika, illustrator.
Identifiers: Canadiana (print) 20200326732 | Canadiana (ebook) 20200326740 | ISBN 9781773214849 (hardcover) | ISBN 9781773214863 (HTML) | ISBN 9781773214870 (PDF) | ISBN 9781773214887 (Kindle)
Classification: LCC PS8607.E2363 A615 2021 | DDC jC813/.6—dc23

Published in the U.S.A. by Annick Press (U.S.) Ltd.
Distributed in Canada by University of Toronto Press.
Distributed in the U.S.A. by Publishers Group West.

Printed in China

annickpress.com
erikaim.com

Also available as an e-book. Please visit annickpress.com/ebooks for more details.

31192022151557